BRAND NEW BABY

Bob Graham

WALKER BOOKS
LONDON

First published 1989 by Walker Books Ltd
as *Waiting for the New Baby, Visiting the New Baby,*
Bringing Home the New Baby and *Getting to Know the New Baby*

This edition published 1992

© 1989 Blackbird Design

Printed and bound in Hong Kong by
Sheck Wah Tong Printing Press Ltd

British Library Cataloguing in Publication Data
A catalogue record for this title is available
from the British Library.
ISBN 0-7445-2309-5

THIS WALKER BOOK BELONGS TO:

_____

_____

_____

_____

Contents

WAITING FOR
the new baby

Mrs Arnold is going to have a brand new baby. She wears dresses as big as tents.

Edward Arnold wears a large box.

Wendy Arnold wears her mum's old
trousers. When the box and the
trousers collide . . .

there is trouble in the Arnold house!

Edward cries, but it's all noise and
no tears.

"Don't be so rough with your brother,"
says Mr Arnold.

Mum bounces Edward on her knee to
help his smile along.

And she needs some help to get out
of the chair.

Dad helps too, as he irons the
tiny clothes that have begun
to appear.

"They're dolls' clothes," says Wendy.
"No, they're baby clothes," says
Mr Arnold.

Sometimes Wendy and Edward pretend
that the new baby has already come.

They wash it,   change its nappy

and feed it on leaves and mud and lots
of watery tea.

"What shall we call the new baby
when she comes?" asks Wendy.
"She may be a boy," says Mum.

"Oh," says Wendy.
"Walter!" says Edward. "Call him
Walter!"

When they sit quietly, they can
feel the new baby moving.

"Hello, Walter," says Wendy.
"Hello, Walter," says Edward.

VISITING
the new baby

Edward and Wendy Arnold are
dressed up as Bat King and
Wonderwoman.

They are going to the hospital
to see their new baby brother
for the first time.

Edward is very excited. He has brought his two best toys.

They are presents for the new
baby, Walter.

But baby Walter looks like he
won't need toys for some time.

He is very small, and pink, and
fast asleep.

"He's like a toy," says Wendy.

"Will he wake up?"

"Such tiny hands," says Dad, "and he looks like Edward."

"Where *is* Edward?"
"He's hiding under the bed with
his silly presents," says Wendy.

"Come up, Edward. Come and
meet Walter . . . and bring your
presents with you."

"They're much too big for baby
Walter," says Wendy.

"They're your best toys! That's
kind of you, Edward," says Mum.

"And I'm sure Walter will look
at them when he wakes up."

"Would you like to hold your
new brother?" asks Mum.
"He looks like he might break,"
says Edward.

"He's still asleep," says Wendy.
Edward is saved by the bell!
It's time to go home.

"Are you quite sure you didn't
want to hold him?" asks Dad.

"When he comes home," says
Edward. "I'll try him when
he comes home."

BRINGING HOME
the new baby

Edward Arnold misses his mum.
So does his sister Wendy.

Their mum is waiting to leave
hospital with the new baby.

Dad is still at home, busy
cleaning up.

He wants everything neat and
tidy for Mum and baby Walter.

Wendy and her brother aren't
helping at all. They're playing
a game called "houses".

When it's time to go to the
hospital, they're still
arranging the furniture.

Wendy and Edward don't like
going to the hospital – it smells
of medicine and floor polish.

It's nice to see Mum again, but
they're not impressed by Walter.
He doesn't do anything much.

"Aren't you going to talk to the
new baby, Edward?" asks Dad.
"You haven't said a word to him yet."

Edward just takes his boat and his bat
car. They were meant to be presents,
but Walter doesn't seem interested.

Mr Arnold takes Mrs Arnold's bag.
The nurse carries baby Walter.

Wendy thinks Walter looks a bit
like a sleeping prune.

In the bus, Walter suddenly wakes up.

He struggles and curls his fingers.

His face changes colour, and . . .

Walter burps very loudly.

"Wow!" says Wendy.
"Not bad!" says Edward.
It's the most interesting thing
Walter has ever done!

When they get home, Grandma is
waiting to help with the baby.
"Anyone for tea and cake?" she says.

"Not for the baby!" says Edward.
"Not for Walter. He's just made the
biggest burp you've ever heard!"

GETTING TO KNOW
the new baby

Here is Wendy Arnold, her brother
Edward and the new baby, Walter.

The trouble with a new baby is that
Mum and Dad never have time for
anything else.

They manage to find time to bath
Walter and to watch him kick and
suck his fists...

but they have no time to help with
pyjamas, the way they used to.

In fact, Mum is always either feeding
the baby or washing or ironing...

or sleeping. She falls asleep a lot
when she's not with baby Walter.

Baby Walter sleeps a lot too.
So games have to be played very

very quietly, even when they are
very very exciting.

But when Edward and his sister are
in *their* beds and fast asleep,

Walter can wake up and make as much
noise as he likes…or so it seems.

In the mornings Walter is much
more likeable.

Wendy and Edward are getting used
to their baby brother. They even help
when he needs his nappy changed.

And every day Walter does new things.

Some days, baby Walter looks
at Wendy and Edward and smiles
as if he knows who they are.

Now Mum and Dad have more time
to play games.

And these days, baby Walter almost
seems part of the family!

Bob Graham was born in 1942. Apart from a year in Manchester (where his daughter Naomi was born), he has spent most of his life in Sydney and Melbourne, Australia. He started illustrating children's books quite late, during a prolonged spell off work due to illness, and his first picture book, *Pete and Roland*, was published in 1981. Since then he has written and illustrated numerous stories of family life, including the Walker titles *The Red Woollen Blanket*, *Has Anyone Here Seen William?*, *Grandad's Magic*, *Brand New Baby* and *Rose Meets Mr Wintergarten* – most of which are based on incidents from his own childhood or that of his two children.

Rose Meets Mr Wintergarten
by Bob Graham

All the children are afraid of mean Mr Wintergarten. His garden is grey and sunless and it is guarded, they say, by a dog like a wolf and a saltwater crocodile. Next door, by contrast, the Summers' garden is a playground of happiness and flowers. So when Rose Summers goes to get her ball back and meets old Mr Wintergarten, the effect is simply dynamic!

Bob Graham's latest picture book is a charming modern fairy tale in the tradition of *The Selfish Giant*.

0-7445-2115-7   £7.99 (hardback only)

For more Bob Graham titles in paperback, please turn the page.